Cosmic Chickens

by Ned Delaney

HARPER & ROW, PUBLISHERS

Library of Congress Cataloging-in-Publication Data
Delaney, Ned.
    Cosmic chickens.

    Summary: Three chickens from outer space help
Hank save his farm from the greedy Mr. Sneezle.
    [1. Chickens—Fiction.   2. Farm life—Fiction.
3. Science fiction]   I. Title.
PZ7.D3732Co 1987   [E]   86-19398
ISBN 0-06-021583-6
ISBN 0-06-021584-4 (lib. bdg.)

For Judy Ambler,
and in remembrance of
Grunion Manor,
Essex, Massachusetts

Hank the farmer had a hard row to hoe. His barn had collapsed. His well had run dry. His mule had arthritis and his chickens had insomnia.

Worst of all, Mr. Sneezle wanted back every last cent Hank had borrowed from the bank to buy his tumbledown farm.

Today, like every day, Hank did his chores. He milked Bessie. Only a few drops squirted into the bucket.

"Dang it," muttered Hank. "That wouldn't even lighten a cup of coffee."

Hank harvested his vegetables.
His corn looked like pickles.

His tomatoes were no bigger
than jelly beans,

and his squash were the size of peanuts.

8

"Dang it," groaned Hank. "I knew I should have planted petunias."

Hank stuffed his vegetables into his pocket and ambled across the field. Toro caught sight of Hank. Toro snorted and charged. Hank hurried. But not fast enough.

"Dang it!" hollered Hank. "I knew I should have raised turkeys."

Mr. Sneezle's limousine skidded across the barnyard.

"That's just like you, Hank," scolded Mr. Sneezle. "Sleeping in the sun when you should be farming! I've come for my money."

Hank dug into his pockets. There was only lint.

"Don't have it, eh?" snarled Mr. Sneezle. "Hank, you have twenty-four hours to raise my $1,951.02 or I tear down your farm and stick up a video games factory.

"To the bank, Raoul," Mr. Sneezle ordered his chauffeur, and the limousine roared off in a cloud of dust.

Hank tore into his farmhouse.
He shook his piggy bank.

He peered into the safe
behind the painting
of his Uncle Moe.

He searched under his mattress.

He had $2.00 to his name.

"Golly," he murmured. "I may be a bad farmer, but
I love my farm. What in the world will I do?"

Hank couldn't eat his dinner that night. He pulled on his pajamas, brushed his teeth, and crawled into bed. He tossed and turned in his sleep.

Suddenly, there was an earthshaking explosion. The whole sky lit up like the Fourth of July.

"Dang lightning bugs," Hank grumbled. He tucked his beard under his blanket and began to snore.

Early the next morning, Hank swung open the chicken coop gate.

"Gee whillikers!" he exclaimed.

There, in the middle of the chicken coop, was a flying saucer.

"Citizen of planet Earth, I believe," said the most fantastic-looking chicken Hank had ever seen.

"Hank the farmer, I presume," said a second odd-looking chicken as it flapped out of the saucer.

A third extraordinary chicken stuck its head out of a porthole. "Our information from the discombobulator reveals you are about to lose your farm to a Sneezle," it said.

"How—how—how do you know my name? And about my farm?" stammered Hank. "Is this Mr. Sneezle's trick?"

"Hank, let us introduce ourselves," said the first chicken. "I'm Zirk."

"I'm Quirk," said the second chicken.

"I'm Irk," said the third.

"Pleased to make your acquaintance," said Hank, shaking their wings.

"We are chickens from the planet Koog," explained Zirk. "We have come to save your farm."

"Jeepers creepers," marveled Hank. "No little green men in outer space—just chickens!"

"Snap out of it, Hank," said Zirk. "We've got a lot of work to do if we're going to out-sneezle the Sneezle. And we have only six hours left."

The three cosmic chickens rummaged through the attic,

poked through the cellar,

and scrounged through the barn.

They loaded a ton of junk into Hank's cart, hitched up the mule, and set off for town.

In the marketplace, Hank nudged his cart between the organ-grinder and the man selling shoelaces. The chickens draped a sign on his mule. It read: MY CHICKEN WILL GUESS YOUR WEIGHT!

"A *chicken* couldn't guess *my* weight," snorted the mayor, pushing his way into line.

"Your Honor," announced Hank, "there's $2.00 in my pocket that says *my* chicken can."

"A fool and his money are soon parted," snickered the mayor, stepping up to have Irk guess his weight.

Irk eyeballed the mayor from head to toe. He started scratching for each pound the mayor weighed. He scratched 199 times.

"Here's your money, wiseguy!" huffed the mayor, stomping off.

Hundreds of townspeople waited in line to have the chicken guess their weight. Irk scratched until his leg ached. By the time the last astonished person had walked away, Hank was a richer farmer.

"It's only a drop in the bucket compared to what I owe Mr. Sneezle," Hank groused.

"Don't get your feathers ruffled yet, Hank," Zirk comforted him.

A new sign was tacked onto Hank's cart. It read:
FOR $3.50 MY CHICKEN WILL GUESS WHAT'S IN
YOUR POCKETS! GUARANTEED.

"Impossible!" scoffed the mayor, shoving his way
through the mob. "Now I can get my two bucks back."

Zirk stared very hard at the mayor. He whispered
something to Hank.

"My chicken says," proclaimed Hank, "that there is
something round in your pocket. It is silver and ticking."

"Aww," pooh-poohed the mayor. "Everyone in town
knows I carry a pocket watch."

Zirk whispered something else to Hank.

"My chicken says there is a letter in your coat pocket,"
said Hank. "It is addressed to Mademoiselle Foo-Foo.
It says..."

"That's enough!" blurted the red-faced mayor, handing
over his money.

Zirk guessed many things in many pockets. Every
guess was right.

"506.50," Zirk informed Hank as he piled the money in Hank's arms.

"Still $606.06 short," muttered Hank. "And only half an hour to go."

There's still a trick or two left up our sleeves, Hank," clucked Zirk.

The chickens made a wigwam out of blankets and hung up one last sign. It read: GURU CHICKEN WILL PEEK INTO YOUR FUTURE FOR ONLY $1.00!

A huge crowd gathered, and before long a line stretched down Main Street.

"Hurry, hurry," hollered the mayor as he cut into the front of the line. "I've just got to talk to that chicken!"

Hank ushered the mayor into the tent.

"Tell me," begged the mayor. "Will I win the election? Do I *have* to kiss babies? Does Foo-Foo really love me?"

Quirk peered into the mayor's future. It did not look bright. People in line heard Quirk's mournful clucking and the mayor's moans of dismay.

When the mayor finally emerged, no one was left in line to have a fortune told.

"My twenty-four hours are up and we've made only
one measly dollar more," groaned Hank.

Hank sold his cart full of junk to the mayor. The mayor was worried he'd need another job if the chicken was right about the election.

"Another $53.03," said Zirk.

"But I still need $552.03," sighed Hank as he led the three cosmic chickens home on his mule.

Back at the saucer, the discombobulator light was
blinking. It was a message from the Boss Chicken
on Koog.

"Gub fot!" cursed Zirk. "The Boss wants us back,
pronto."

"We have to help a Martian make a mountain,"
said Irk, buttoning up the hatch.

"Out of a molehill," added Quirk, switching on the
antigravity gizmo.

"Don't fret over the Sneezle, Hank," consoled Zirk
"We'll be back in half a phizpul to get you out of
your jam."

As Hank scuffed his toe in the barnyard dust, the
saucer became a speck in the sky.

Suddenly, Mr. Sneezle roared up in his limousine.
"Hank!" he bellowed. "I've got to have those chickens!"

"Chickens?" asked Hank. "*My* chickens that can't
sleep and won't lay eggs?"

"How much will you sell them for?" demanded
Mr. Sneezle, digging into his pockets. "$500? $650?
$659? Name your price, Hank."

Hank had a brainstorm.

"My chickens are expensive," he said calmly.

"How much?" cried Mr. Sneezle. "$750? $999?"

"My chickens cost $1,951.02," said Hank.

"Hoo boy, that's steep," said Mr. Sneezle. "But here, take this. It ought to cover your chickens."

Mr. Sneezle slapped the deed to the farm in Hank's palm.

Hank fetched an armful of very expensive chickens from the coop and handed them over to Mr. Sneezle.

"My little darlings," cooed Mr. Sneezle as he gingerly buckled seat belts around his three hens.

"Hank, with these magical chickens you could have been a billionaire," sneered Mr. Sneezle. "But now you'll always be a farmer. So long, peabrain!"

Hank watched the limousine disappear down the road.

"A fool and his money are soon parted," he thought.

Hank still had all that money the cosmic chickens had raised for him. He used it to fix his barn,

dig a new well,

cure his mule's arthritis,

and buy brand-new chickens that slept soundly at night.

There was even enough money to plant petunias
around the farmhouse.

It was a fine farm. Hank was in seventh heaven.

46

A year later, Hank unfolded the morning paper
and read:

TATTLER 5¢

SNEEZE SNARED!

For bamboozling innocent folks with his chicken fortune-telling scheme, Egbert Sneeze was locked behind bars yesterday. The key was thrown away for good measure.

A smile as big as the moon spread across Hank's face.